SANTA
in the SUMMER

Written by Jay Schleifer

Art by Debbie Hefke

North Pole Stories

For Susan

With special thanks to Debbie Hefke
for bringing Summer Santa to life.

Copyright © 2015 by Jay Schleifer
Cover & illustrations by: Debbie Hefke

ISBN-13: 978-1517493318

Email: NorthPoleStories@gmail.com
Website: www.SantaintheSummer.com

Did you ever wonder what Santa does in the summer?

We know what he does in the winter.

He brings toys to girls and boys.

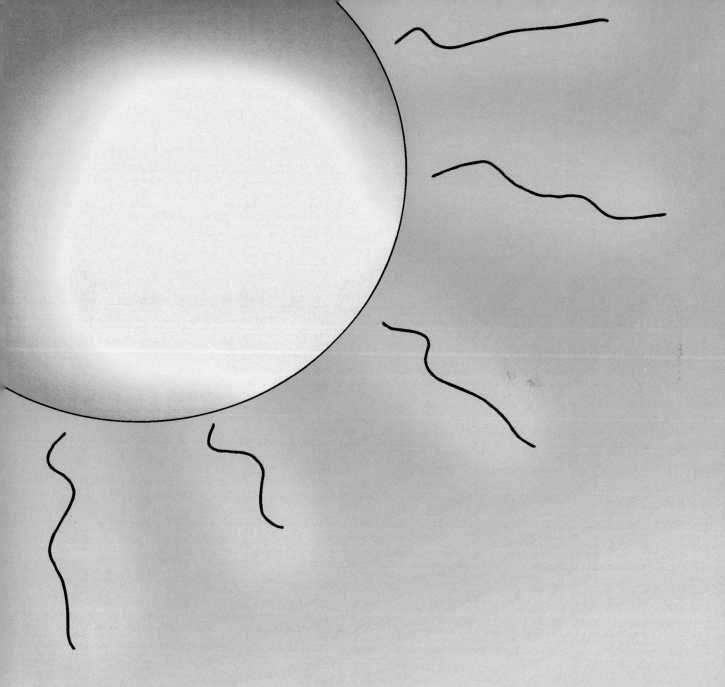

But what about when the weather is fine
and the sun is ... **HOT**!

Does he still drag around that big bag?

Does he still get around in a sleigh when there's no ice and snow to ride on?

Just what DOES Santa do in the summer?

Maybe he goes to the beach ... and builds a snowman out of sand.

Maybe he goes to the country....
and picks *delicious* berries!

Maybe he goes sightseeing in faraway places.

Mt. Rushmore

Eiffel
Tower

Big
Ben

Statue of
Liberty

Great Wall of China

Or does he catch up on his sleep because, in the winter, he's up all night?

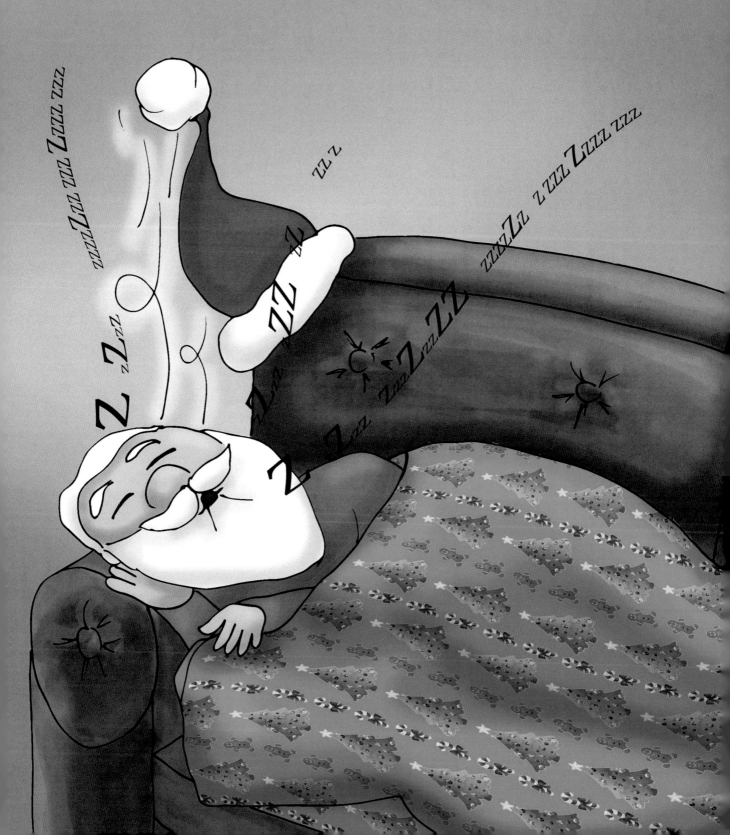

Maybe Mrs. Claus sends Santa to day camp...

...since he's such a BIG KID!

Or maybe Santa just goes out in the back yard and...

...enjoys a big, sloppy burger fresh off the grill.

Whatever he does, you can be sure Santa spends some of his summer helping others ...

...because love is a gift you can give all year long.

So now that you know some things Santa does in the summer.

Can you find him?

Turn the next page.

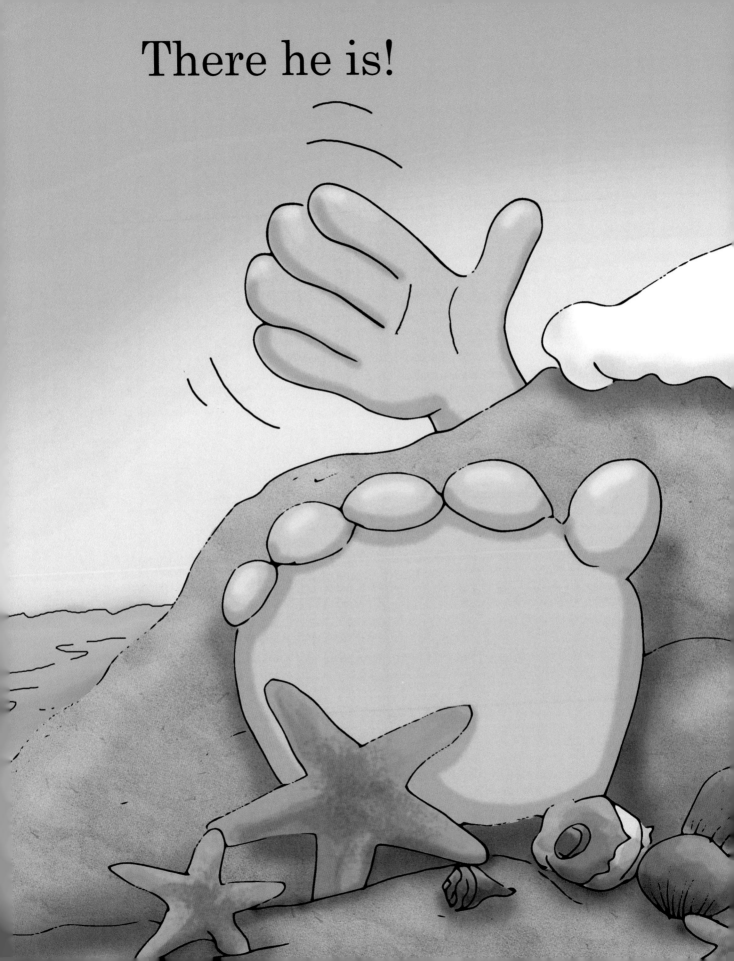

But even if you don't see Santa in the summer...

...don't worry, because...

You'll see him in the winter!

Merry Christmas!

Things to Talk About

Santa in the Summer is primarily a fun book, but there are important learnings that can be gained from reading it as well. You might want to try discussing these questions with your youngsters:

1. What are some of the things Santa loves to do in the summer? What are your favorite things to do in the summer? Which do you like most? Why?

2. What does Santa do in the summer that helps others? What are some things you could do to help others?

3. Santa goes sightseeing to interesting places around the world. Have you heard of any of the places he goes? Ask your parents about them or have someone help you find out about them in books or on the Internet. Also, see where they are on a world map, compared to where you are. In what ways would you travel to get there?

4. The book tells what Santa likes to do when he's not around us. Think of your favorite cartoon characters. What do you think they are like when you don't see them? What do they like to do? Now think of some people you know but don't see all the time? What do you think their lives are like?

About the Author

Jay Schleifer, a former teacher, served 15 years as a writer, editor and product developer with the *Weekly Reader* Company, publisher of the world's most read classroom newspapers. He has authored 40 books for young readers and teens. Jay lives in Florida with his wife Susan, also an author, and their cocker spaniel, Sidney, who is not an author but enjoys chicken snacks and time in the local dog park.

About North Pole Stories

Santa in the Summer is the first book of this new series, designed to employ one of childhood's most familiar and beloved characters, Santa Claus, along with his human and animal family and friends, to explore the world and new experiences beyond their traditional holiday time boundaries.

If you'd like to be kept informed as new books become available, visit *SantaintheSummer.com* or write us at North Pole Stories, 14611 Southern Blvd, P.O. Box 591, Loxahatchee, FL 33470.

Made in the USA
Middletown, DE
04 December 2019